THE SECRET
DAKOTA KING

#3 Two-Wheeled Terror

Jake MacKenzie

SCHOLASTIC INC.
New York Toronto London Auckland Sydney

Design and Illustration: **Hal Aber**

Cover Illustration: **Bill Purdom**

Photos: **Neal Edwards**

Scholastic Books are available at special discounts for quantity purchases for use as premiums, promotional items, retail sales through specialty market outlets, etc. For details contact: Special Sales Manager, Scholastic Inc., 730 Broadway, New York, NY 10003.

ISBN 0-590-40751-1

12 11 10 9 8 7 6 5 4 3 2 1   8 9/8 0 1 2 3/9

Printed in the U.S.A.   28

First Scholastic printing, January 1988

"I'm outta here, Boss!"

DAKOTA KING
AGENT AT LARGE

Hi Boss,

Here's one file I know you've been waiting for, since you actually asked me to take on this case of THE TWO-WHEELED TERROR. As you and all other Z.O.O. agents will see, the theft of your nephew Alex's bike led Lorgh Gonh and me straight to something a lot bigger. I guess you asked me to check out the bike theft because you suspected it was connected with a matter that the new espionage laws wouldn't allow the Z.O.O. to touch. But even you couldn't have known what you were getting me into.

Can't stay to help you put all the clues in this file together to find out what the crime was and who committed it. I'm heading out west. Until next time....

I'm outta here, Boss!

D K

3

ZONE OPERATIONS ORGANIZATION
9009 Incognito Drive Arlington, Virginia   90909
703-555-9009   TELEX: 99-9009

MEMORANDUM

TO: All agents in the Z.O.O. (Zone Operations
  Organization)
FROM: The Zookeeper
CONCERNING: The Dakota King File

TWO-WHEELED TERROR

In his usual style, Dakota King—his own favorite
agent-at-large—has left us with an unfinished case.
Once again, he claims that everything we need to
solve the case is right here, in what he laughingly
refers to as a "file."

This time around, DK didn't stumble onto the case.
He got involved because I asked him to look into a
family matter for me. As most of you know, King and
his associate, Longh Gonh, were once two of our best
agents. When King decided that government
bureaucracy was cramping his style, he left the
agency and started his own business. You all know
what it's called—Disappearing Inc. Gonh joined him

in this scheme, and ever since, we've had to deal with the two of them on a free-lance basis.

The family matter, which involves my teenage nephew, is not important. King took care of that in his usual flamboyant manner. What is important is his claim that my nephew's problem led him to a discovery of some illegal matters in which he says the Z.O.O. will be interested.

I'm sure that DK is right, but I can't interrupt my busy schedule to go through this messy collection of police data, drawings, transcripts, computer messages, memos, and who knows what else to figure out what he discovered. Therefore, I'm sending this dossier to all agents. THAT MEANS YOU! Copies of everything DK sent me are here. I want you to read it all, make some sense out of it, and let me know **who has committed a crime—and what the crime was.**

For those of you not familiar with Dakota's methods, I've included the profile from his personnel folder.

Good luck, agents—you'll need it!

The Zookeeper

ZONE OPERATIONS ORGANIZATION

CONFIDENTIAL PROFILE REPORT

Subject: Dakota King
Age: Unrecorded
Height: 6' 3"
Distinguishing marks: Eagle tattoo on inside of left wrist
Address: General Post Office Every Major City
Home Base: Redd Cliff, Colorado
Contact Base: The Z.O.O.
Partner and Contact: Longh Gonh (separate profile on file), Disappearing Inc. agent
Occupation: Agent-at-large for own agency, Disappearing Inc.
Services valued by Organization: Investigative skills used in studies of unexplained events, uncharted territories, unsolved mysteries of the world.
Special Interests: Freedom and justice for all—especially Dakota King; fine art and illustration (published works of Dakota King's own art include: Dakota King's Sketchbook, King's Ransom: Collected Drawings of Dakota King, and Dakota!); magic (King is a world-renowned magician known for contributing

numerous tricks and illusions to master magicians on all continents).

Education: Life experience. Spent boyhood traveling with anthropologist parents who found him living with the Kayuga Indians in Death Valley and adopted him when he was a small boy. Travels exposed him to numerous tribal cultures in this country and all over the world.

While living with the Kayuga, he received survival training, learned to read nature's danger signals, learned to use the celestial bodies, the oceans, rivers, and earth's vibrations as means of predicting events and even changing events. Acclaimed expert in the customs and mystical ceremonies of American Indian tribes. Followed and lived with Gypsy tribes in Hungary, Italy, and throughout Europe. Accepted and welcomed by all Gypsy tribes on every continent as adopted son of Zolan, King of the Gypsies. No stranger to the Himalayas and the unnumbered villages and uncharted regions which lay hidden on the summits, in the valleys, and in the caves of these mysterious mountains. Recognized expert in knowledge of great impostors of the 18th, 19th, and 20th centuries.

Experience: Consultant to government intelligence agencies in the use of illusion for diversion tactics to be used as alternatives to weapons. References available on request from members of the private sector who have used his services for finding lost treasures and tracing family fortunes.

Hobbies: Flying, race car driving, D & D, art, inventing communication devices, and experiencing life.

ARCADIA POLICE DEPARTMENT
STOLEN PROPERTY REPORT

NAME Walker, Arthur J.

ADDRESS 11 Comet Drive

HOME TELEPHONE 555-4190   **DATE** 29 July

DESCRIPTION OF STOLEN PROPERTY One (1) red Riviera racing bicycle, purchased 28 May, delivered 27 July.

ESTIMATED VALUE OF PROPERTY $782

DATE AND TIME OF THEFT Overnight, 28–29 July, probably between midnight and 6 a.m.

RECONSTRUCT OCCURRENCE, INCLUDING METHOD OF ENTRY AND ESCAPE Perpetrator apparently used one or more tools to break open lock of garage door. Complainant reports no property missing except one bike. Garage door was left open. In our investigation of the premises, we discovered a small tool bag containing wrenches and screwdrivers, **apparently all metric in size.** Except for broken lock, no property damage discovered. Complainant has no suggestions about identity of perpetrator. Bike ID number is registered with dealer, but not with Arcadia P.D. Complainant's son said he was "going to get around to that" today.

OFFICERS FILING THIS REPORT

Patrol Officer Joseph Venerdi   Patrol Officer Jennifer Smith

COMPUTER REPORT

TO: DAKOTA KING

FROM: THE ZOOKEEPER

CONCERNING: POLICE REPORT OF STOLEN PROPERTY

THE Z.O.O. COMMUNICATIONS DIVISION HAS JUST TELEMAILED A COPY OF A STOLEN PROPERTY REPORT FROM THE ARCADIA POLICE DEPARTMENT. IT SHOULD BE SITTING IN YOUR TELEPRINTER RIGHT NOW. A STOLEN BICYCLE IS NOT THE SORT OF THING THE Z.O.O. WOULD NORMALLY DEVOTE TIME TO. BUT THE OWNER OF THE BIKE IS MY SISTER'S SON, AND I TOLD HIM I'D LOOK INTO THE MATTER FOR HIM.

ONE OF OUR AGENTS DID LOOK INTO IT, AND WHAT SHE FOUND MAKES IT NECESSARY FOR ME TO PASS THE CASE ON TO A PRIVATE AGENCY, SUCH AS DISAPPEARING INC. AS YOU KNOW, RECENT CONGRESSIONAL HEARINGS HAVE LED TO A NEW SERIES OF RESTRICTIONS ON VARIOUS AGENCIES. WE ARE NO LONGER ALLOWED TO INVESTIGATE MATTERS

THAT ARE STRICTLY DOMESTIC IN NATURE.
OUR AGENT TRACED THE THEFT OF THE BIKE
TO AN ARCADIA COMPANY CALLED CADENCE
PROPERTIES. AT THAT POINT, WE HAD TO
BACK OUT OF THE CASE.

I'M DEPENDING ON YOU TO FIND OUT WHY
A LARGE CORPORATION WOULD WANT MY
NEPHEW'S BIKE. ALEX, BY THE WAY, THINKS
I'M IN THE "SECURITY" BUSINESS. YOU ARE
NOT TO SAY ANYTHING THAT WOULD LEAD
HIM TO BELIEVE OTHERWISE.

END OF REPORT

Dakota King's
Microdiary Entry #1
Re: <u>Two-Wheeled Terror</u>

A stolen bike, Boss? Usually your requests are a little more high-level than that, like the top-secret alloy I dug up for you last time around. But if you guys can't track down your own nephew's missing wheels—well, somebody's gotta help.

That police report you sent was sketchy, but I suspect I'll fill in the pictures pretty fast with a little advanced technology. Like this microrecorder I invented for instance. Since I do a lot of my best investigative thinking while I'm riding my bike, I put the microrecorder in a stopwatch around my neck. I'll be able to talk to you at the same time that I'm pedaling my daily fifty miles on the road.

How's that for a coincidence? A month ago I decided that the next thing I had to master was long-distance biking. For the past four weeks, I've been thinking about nothing but cycling. Then your request pops up on my computer screen. For a change, I get to combine a little business with a little sport. Not bad.

I'm training for the bike race that's being held right here in Arcadia next week. So, if you hear some huffing on this tape, just chalk it up to my not being in absolutely perfect physical condition . . . yet.

After I found your message on my computer, the first thing I did was talk it over with Longh Gonh. Longh's unshakable calm and general levelheadedness always help me get an angle on a new assignment. Longh said he'd see what he could find out about Cadence Properties, while I talked to the police.

When I finish my fifty miles this morning, I have an appointment to talk with Patrol Officer Venerdi. He might have some information that doesn't appear in the report. It must have been tough on your nephew Alex, having his bike stolen two days after he got it. I'll be talking to him soon to see what he can tell me.

Don't worry, Boss, I won't tell Alex what you do for a living. (Sometimes *I'm* not even sure what that is.) No, I won't tell him you put me on the case. I'll just talk to him as a fellow bike racer and get him to tell me everything I need to know.

Longh and I looked over your agent's report on her investigation into the stolen bike. (As requested, I returned the report to you right away.) My favorite part is that Alex himself spotted **a suspicious car** in his neighborhood and was smart enough to copy down the license number. I haven't even met the kid yet, but I like him already.

Anyway, the way I get it, the Z.O.O. crew traced the license number—CP-804—to Cadence Properties. So I figure you have some information about Cadence that you can't pass on to me. Because of the new regulations, you have to keep me in the dark about it, even though you know I'm going to find it out. (When Longh Gonh and I work together, Boss, we find *everything* out. You know that.)

My odometer reads 49.4 miles. I'm off for a quick shower and a little talk with Officer Venerdi. I'll keep you posted on late-breaking developments.

Dakota King's
Microdiary Entry #2
Re: Two-Wheeled Terror

Before I took off for the police station, I gave the stolen property report another look. The officers must have had a lot on their minds that day, none of it having to do with stolen bicycles. Not a word about footprints, tire tracks, or fingerprints. What do those people get paid for, anyway?

By now, of course, any trace of the thief would be gone. Even so, I decided that I'd go have a look at the premises after I talked with Officer Venerdi.

The desk sergeant directed me to a small meeting room, where I waited for Officer Venerdi. When he walked down the hall I clicked on my microrecorder, still hidden in my stopwatch.

****

TRANSCRIPT

DK: Thanks for agreeing to talk to me, Officer Venerdi. I'll only take a few minutes of your time.

JV: No trouble. Are you with the insurance company?

DK: No, not exactly.

JV: Oh, a family lawyer, then?

DK: Something like that. I'm representing the Walker family.

JV: I'm not sure I can tell you anything more than I wrote in the official report.

DK: Probably not. Would you just describe the scene you found when you arrived?

JV: Sure. The garage door was open. Inside, there were a car and three bikes. One bike belonged to Mrs. Walker, one was her daughter Michelle's, and one was Alex's.

DK: I thought it was Alex's bike that was stolen.

JV: His brand-new bike was stolen. This was his old bike.

DK: So the thief took only one bike. And nothing else was missing?

JV: I had Mr. and Mrs. Walker check everything over very carefully. They were sure nothing was missing except the new bike.

DK: How did the thief get into the garage?

JV: The lock had been jimmied open. It was a very clean job. I'd say it was done by a professional.

DK: Not a kid from the neighborhood?

JV: Asolutely not. The lock looked as though it had been handled by a surgeon. We found a tool bag nearby, but I can't say if any of the tools in it were used on the door. We couldn't get a usable fingerprint from any part of the bag.

DK: Could I see that bag?

JV: I don't see why not. It's right here in this cabinet. Look.

[HE SHOWED ME A CLOTH TOOL KIT, SMALL ENOUGH TO FIT INTO A GLOVE COMPARTMENT. THE ZIPPER-PULL HAD A **LEATHER SQUARE** HANGING FROM IT, LIKE THOSE THINGS PEOPLE ATTACH TO THEIR CAR KEYS, ONLY BIGGER. THE LEATHER HAD SOMETHING PRINTED ON IT, BUT IT WAS **TORN IN HALF.**]

DK: WAS THIS TAG TORN LIKE THIS WHEN YOU FOUND IT?

JV: IT LOOKED EXACTLY THE WAY IT DOES NOW.

DK: DID YOU SEE FOOTPRINTS OR TIRE TRACKS IN THE GARAGE AREA?

JV: WE LOOKED AROUND, BUT WE DIDN'T FIND ANYTHING.

DK: DIDN'T ALEX SAY ANYTHING TO YOU ABOUT THAT SUSPICIOUS-LOOKING CAR THAT SLOWED DOWN AND WATCHED HIM GO UP HIS DRIVEWAY?

JV: OH, THAT SILVER BMW? WELL, THAT'S HARDLY SIGNIFICANT. I MEAN, JUST THE FACT THAT THE CAR SLOWED DOWN. ANYWAY, BIKE THIEVES DON'T DRIVE EXPENSIVE CARS LIKE THAT—NOT THE ONES WE KNOW, ANYWAY. [HE LAUGHED.]

DK: THANKS, OFFICER VENERDI. YOU'VE BEEN VERY HELPFUL.

JV: ANY TIME.

END OF TRANSCRIPT

****

Dakota King's
Microdiary Entry #3
Re: Two-Wheeled Terror

The tool kit didn't mean anything to me until I did some snooping outside of Alex's house. I rang the doorbell first, ready to tell anyone who answered that I was from the insurance company. Since no one was home, I just looked around.

I wasn't looking for anything in particular, but I thought the police might have missed something. Sure enough, within thirty seconds I found a clue. I could see it from ten feet away, right there under a bush near the garage door. It was the other half of the torn leather piece from the tool kit. Take a look.

I put the leather tag in my pocket and pedaled away. I was trying to come up with a plan for "acci-

CLUE #1

STRAUSS TOOLS
AELBRECHTSKADE 17
1748 KV
AMSTERDAM, HOLLAND

dentally" bumping into Alex Walker so we could talk about his stolen bike.

The plan became unnecessary when we met up at a stoplight and started talking bike talk. Alex had a dozen questions about the custom racer I had designed. Pretty soon we were heavy into derailleurs, sprockets, and cables. In no time, he told me all about what happened to his own wheels. And also in no time, Boss, he told me he'd already figured out that you had sent me to talk to him. Pretty sharp kid.

I told him that would have to remain a secret between us, and he said it would. Now he considers himself an undercover agent. He told me you're in the security business, but he seems to believe that you sell burglar alarms or something. I'd love to be around some day when you're talking to your relatives about your work, Boss. Pencil me in for the next family reunion, will you?

Here's the background Alex gave me about his bike. He ordered it on May 28th at Shaw's Cycle Shop on Clemens Street. For two months, he stayed up nights thinking about that bike. Then, last Thursday, he stopped in at Shaw's, the way he did almost every afternoon. Mr. Shaw told him the shipment of bikes would be at the airport on Monday, and Alex could pick up his bike at the store on Tuesday.

At this point, Alex wasn't about to wait one more day than he had to. So he whined and wheedled until Shaw gave in. He agreed to let Alex go with him to accept the shipment, then ride his bike home from the airport.

Sounds innocent enough. But Alex noticed some strange things that day and the next . . . It was time to click on my stopwatch and get the facts on tape for you, Boss. I'll let Alex tell about what happened.

****

TRANSCRIPT

DK: How did you get to the airport?

AW: We rode in Mr. Shaw's van. He was picking up six bikes. Five, without mine. It was a strange ride, though.

DK: Strange? In what way?

AW: Mr. Shaw seemed to be, I don't know, nervous or something. I've known him for a long time. And I've never seen him fidgety, like he was that day. He got worse when we got to the customs desk.

DK: What did he do there?

AW: He kept looking around, as though he thought someone was watching him. He yelled at one of the customs guys for keeping us waiting.

DK: Did you have to wait long?

AW: Just a few minutes. There were some newspaper people there, though, and I think that made Mr. Shaw even more nervous.

DK: Reporters? Why were they there?

AW: Some Italian movie star and his wife were coming into the country. Reporters and photographers were all over the customs area.

DK: So how did you finally get your bike?

AW: Mr. Shaw signed some papers. Then we went outside to a loading dock. There were the six bikes waiting to be picked up. They were in these long, narrow cardboard boxes. We slid five of the

BOXES INTO MR. SHAW'S VAN. THEN WE CUT OPEN THE ONE MARKED "RIVIERA, RED." AND THERE WAS MY BIKE. WELL, ALMOST. WE HAD TO PUT THE HANDLEBARS AND THE PEDALS ON. THAT TOOK JUST A COUPLE OF MINUTES. THEN I WAS READY TO GO.

DK: AND MR. SHAW?

AW: HE SEEMED IN A HURRY TO GET ME OUT OF THERE. HE JUST STOOD THERE BY HIS VAN AND SAID, "BE CAREFUL RIDING HOME." THEN HE SORT OF. . .WAVED AT ME.

DK: AND WHAT DID YOU DO?

AW: ME? I TOOK ONE OF THE BEST SHORT BIKE RIDES EVER. YOU KNOW HOW GREAT IT FEELS TO BE ON A NEW BIKE? THIS WAS ABOUT ELEVEN TIMES GREATER, BECAUSE I'D BEEN WAITING SO LONG. I RODE OUT THROUGH THE TAXI EXIT, THEN HEADED HOME.

DK: HOW LONG A RIDE IS IT?

AW: IT'S ONLY ABOUT FIVE OR SIX MILES, SO I WAS HOME IN TWENTY MINUTES.

DK: WHAT ABOUT THIS SUSPICIOUS CAR I'VE HEARD ABOUT?

AW: OH, UNCLE ULYSSES TOLD YOU ABOUT THAT, HUH?

DK: UNCLE ULYSSES?

AW: WELL, I FIGURED THAT'S WHERE YOU FOUND OUT ABOUT IT. THE POLICE DIDN'T SEEM AT ALL INTERESTED IN HEARING ABOUT THE CAR. I WAS ABOUT TWO BLOCKS FROM MY HOUSE, AND I HAD STOPPED FOR A RED LIGHT. I LOOKED OVER MY SHOULDER TO CHECK THE TRAFFIC BEHIND ME. AND I SAW A CAR STOPPED, ABOUT TWENTY FEET BACK. IT WASN'T DOUBLE-PARKED, OR ANYTHING. IT WAS IN THE MIDDLE OF THE LANE. THEN THE LIGHT CHANGED,

AND I PEDALED ACROSS THE INTERSECTION. I LOOKED BACK, AND THE CAR WAS MOVING.

DK: THIS DOESN'T SOUND VERY SUSPICIOUS TO ME.

AW: WELL, THERE ARE A COUPLE OF THINGS THAT MADE ME FEEL UNCOMFORTABLE. FIRST, THE CAR WAS A SILVER **BMW**. IN MY NEIGHBORHOOD, AN EXPENSIVE CAR LIKE THAT REALLY STANDS OUT. SECOND, THE CAR WAS STILL BEHIND ME WHEN I RODE UP MY DRIVEWAY. IT MOVED SLOWLY PAST MY HOUSE, STOPPED AT THE CORNER, THEN TOOK OFF.

DK: THAT'S A LITTLE MORE SUBSTANTIAL, BUT IT STILL DOESN'T QUALIFY AS SUSPICIOUS.

AW: WAIT, THERE'S MORE. AS THE CAR DROVE PAST MY HOUSE, I HAD A WEIRD FEELING. I WAS SURE I'D SEEN IT **PARKED NEAR THE LOADING DOCK** A HALF-HOUR EARLIER. THAT MIGHT SOUND A LITTLE CRAZY. BUT WHAT HAPPENED THE NEXT DAY MADE ME SURE SOMETHING FISHY WAS GOING ON.

DK: YOU SAW THE CAR AGAIN, DIDN'T YOU?

AW: HOW DID YOU KNOW THAT?

DK: I KNOW YOU GOT THE LICENSE NUMBER. IF YOU DIDN'T COPY IT WHEN THE CAR PASSED YOUR HOUSE, THEN YOU MUST HAVE SEEN IT AGAIN.

AW: VERY GOOD, DAKOTA.

DK: NOT REALLY. IT'S WHAT THEY PAY ME FOR.

AW: ANYWAY, I DID SEE IT, NEAR THE SHOPPING CENTER DOWNTOWN. AND I DID MORE THAN COPY THE LICENSE NUMBER. I DREW A PICTURE.

DK: YOU DREW A PICTURE OF THE CAR? WHY?

AW: NOT THE CAR. THE DRIVER. HE WAS STANDING NEXT TO THE CAR. HE SEEMED TO BE WAITING FOR SOMEBODY, AND I KNOW HE DIDN'T SEE ME. SO

I RODE ACROSS THE STREET AND LOCKED MY BIKE UP IN FRONT OF THE POST OFFICE. THEN I MOVED WITH A CROWD OF PEOPLE UNTIL I WAS DIRECTLY ACROSS FROM THE CAR. THE GUY WAS LOOKING AT THE ENTRANCE TO THE SHOPPING CENTER, SO HE NEVER SAW ME. I GOT A GOOD LOOK AT HIM, THOUGH. AND I DREW THIS PICTURE.

CLUE #2

DK: That's pretty good work, Alex. Where did you learn to draw like this?

AW: I'm just a man of many talents, Dakota.

DK: So you are. Can I borrow this?

AW: Sure. Why?

DK: I want to show it to my partner, Longh Gonh. I like him to know everything I know. He absorbs information differently from the rest of us, so it's always best to show him things instead of telling him about them.

AW: Sounds like an interesting guy.

DK: He is. I'll make sure you meet him.

END OF TRANSCRIPT

****

Dakota King's
Microdiary Entry #4
Re: Two-Wheeled Terror

After I left Alex, I went home to wait for Longh Gonh. I propped Alex's drawing up on the easel Longh uses when the mood for oils and brushes strikes him. (He says it helps him concentrate.)

The guy in Alex's drawing looked pretty sinister. But that didn't make him a bike thief. Besides, I found it hard not to take the same position as the police. Why would a guy in a sixty-thousand-dollar car want some kid's bike, even an expensive one?

The bigger question was, how did I get involved in investigating a bike theft, when even the police offered little hope that the bike would ever be seen again? I was trying to train for a bike race, only a little over a week away. Did I really have the time to go after some bike thief?

I must have been thinking out loud because Longh answered my question. "One creates time for whatever must be done, Dakota," he said quietly.

"Hi, Longh," I said, turning to face the door. "What did you do, float in?"

"Time does not come in a bottle, like milk," he said, ignoring my question. "It is a flexible commodity, which each of us shapes to his own needs."

"Not exactly the way I'd put it," I said, "but

you're right, Longh. Alex is a good kid. It would be a shame if Disappearing Inc. couldn't do something about his missing bike."

"There is also something else that makes it impossible for us to turn our backs on this case," Longh said.

"What's that?"

"The Z.O.O. did not toss this matter at you casually," he said. "The Zookeeper had a reason for putting you on the trail of this missing bike."

"Thanks for reminding me," I said. "Sure, they traced the BMW's license number to a company named Cadence Properties. Then they dropped the case in our laps."

"The Z.O.O. is prohibited from investigating Cadence because of the new government regulations. Those regulations, however, do not stop them from recognizing a suspicious situation when they stumble upon it."

Longh, of course, was referring to the scandal that had recently broken open in Washington. A dozen undercover people had been discovered running their own operations. All for good "patriotic" reasons, of course, but much to the dismay of a handful of Congressional committees.

The Z.O.O. hadn't been included, but the new rules applied to all agencies. Now everyone had to be careful to stick to the letter of the law. If the law didn't give an agency power to pursue a case, they'd better back off.

Or quietly pass it on to a trusty free-lancer.

"So we know something is up at Cadence," I said. "What's our next step?"

"It is time to concentrate, Dakota," Longh said.

I turned around and saw that he was lying on the floor with his eyes closed and his hands clasped over his chest. This is Longh's favorite meditating position. He also uses it when he's thinking about a difficult problem.

"Join me," he said. "Concentrate."

I looked down at him. He looked so peaceful, so in tune with everything. His calmness reminded me that I too can be in tune. So I stretched out on the couch, folded my hands over my chest, and closed my eyes.

"Okay," I said. "What now?"

"Your bike clubs," Longh said. Before I could ask what he was talking about, he went on. "You belong to three of them."

"Sure," I said. "I need all the riding I can get if we're going to ace that race. The people in these clubs ride together once a week. That's about one-third as much riding as I want. So I joined three clubs."

"That is good," Longh said. "And when I have been to these clubs with you, I have noticed something about the bulletin boards in the three clubs."

"Bulletin boards?" I said. "Pretty dull stuff, Longh. What are you getting at?"

"Think, Dakota," he said. "Use the memory skills your Ninja master taught you as a boy."

I drifted into that frame of mind I had learned to adopt from my Ninja master. I though of the game of the stones, through which I learned to develop a memory that astounded kids I met when I came back to this country.

"Think of the second lesson you learned," Longh said.

In the game of the stones, my Ninja master first taught me to remember the contents of a box that held dozens of stones of various colors, shapes, and sizes. When I improved, he taught me the second lesson.

"You have described most of the stones in the

box," my master said. "Now describe the box."

Of course, I couldn't do it. That was the first step in learning Lesson No. 2, which, loosely translated, means, "Don't miss the forest because of the trees."

With my eyes closed, I pictured the bulletin boards, as Longh had suggested. There they were, one by one. Then I saw them all together. Notices about bike trips, safety classes, and subscriptions to biking magazines.

The harder I concentrated, the better I could see the boards. Now I had a close-up view of all three together, something that would have been impossible in the real world.

Suddenly, the zoom lens in my mind moved in on one ad that appeared on all three boards.

CLUE #3

BEFORE YOU MAKE A DECISION ABOUT BUYING A NEW BIKE, CALL US FOR THE DEAL OF THE CENTURY. SHOP AROUND AND GET YOUR BEST PRICE FOR ANY BIKE MADE IN **FRANCE, ENGLAND, OR HOLLAND.**

WE'LL GET IT FOR YOU AT HALF-PRICE. FOR A GUARANTEED 50% DISCOUNT,

CALL: 1-800-555-9121

"Bicycles from France and Holland," I whispered.

"You've done it again," Longh said. "Congratulations."

"You think there's any connection?" I asked.

"It could be just a coincidence," Longh said. "But somehow I doubt that."

Alex's bike had come to the airport from France. The police found a tool bag from Holland near the garage. And now this ad.

Things were beginning to look interesting. They weren't making much sense yet, but they were beginning to look interesting.

Longh left for his pre-dinner five-mile run, and I decided it was time to start gathering information. I sat down at my computer and tapped into my best source—the network of computer hackers I've belonged to for years.

By far the best among them is Zan. Beyond that nickname, I know only two things about her. Her first name is really Alexandra, and she can get me any kind of data on any kind of subject. Zan and I have been "talking" by way of computer for years, although we've never met. In fact, I don't even know where she operates from. I have a hunch that she's somewhere in the Southwest, but I don't have any evidence for that.

Zan won't talk to just anybody. From what she's told me, there are several people she won't talk to at all. That's why she gave me the code name Tarzan, and devised another special code for me. I draw seven "flowers" on the screen, for the seven days of the week. I leave the bud off the one for the day I'm calling her. That's how she knows it's really "Tarzan" who's sending the message.

Since this was Wednesday, the fourth flower had no bud. She responded almost immediately.

*** ***
!!!!!!!

COMPUTER CONVERSATION

● HMM. MY FAVORITE FLOWERS. HELLO, TARZAN. WHY HAVEN'T I HEARD FROM YOU FOR OVER TWO WEEKS?

● HELLO, ZAN. I HAVEN'T BEEN WORKING. I'VE BEEN TRAINING FOR A BIKE RACE.

● YOU MEAN YOU'LL BE IN EVEN BETTER SHAPE THAN BEFORE? IS THAT POSSIBLE? WHAT CAN I DO FOR YOU TONIGHT? I KEEP HOPING IT WILL BE SOMETHING THAT GETS US TO MEET FACE-TO-FACE.

● ONE OF THESE DAYS WE WILL, ZAN. RIGHT NOW I NEED SOME INFO THAT ONLY YOU CAN GET FOR ME.

● THAT'S THE KIND OF THING I LOVE TO HEAR.

● I NEED TO KNOW THREE THINGS. FIRST, I'D LIKE THE NAME OF THE PERSON OR COMPANY THAT HAS RENTED THIS PHONE NUMBER: 800-555-9121. SECOND, GET ME

WHATEVER YOU CAN ABOUT A COMPANY CALLED CADENCE PROPERTIES, WITH HEAD-QUARTERS IN ARCADIA. THIRD, IS THERE ANY CONNECTION BETWEEN THE 800 NUMBER, CADENCE, AND BICYCLES?

- WILL DO. HOW URGENT IS THIS?
- I'M GOING TO BED NOW. ANY TIME TOMORROW WILL BE FINE.
- YOU'LL HAVE IT. SWEET DREAMS.

END OF COMPUTER CONVERSATION

Dakota King's
Microdiary Entry #5
Re: Two-Wheeled Terror

The next morning, I got up before dawn to do my daily fifty. I had a feeling the day was going to be full, and I wanted to get my training in before the crunch.

I planned the ride so I'd end up at Shaw's Cycle Shop. I got there a little after nine o'clock, just in time to see Shaw unlocking the front door. As he saw me riding up to the store, he smiled and called out, "Good morning!"

I locked the bike at a rack in front of the cycle shop and followed Shaw inside. He was a pleasant-looking man, about forty or so. He was in great shape for a guy that age. I pressed the button on my stopwatch and the microrecorder started to work.

****

TRANSCRIPT

DK: MR. SHAW, MY NAME'S DAKOTA KING.

OS: ORVILLE SHAW. [WE SHOOK HANDS.]

DK: I'M A FRIEND OF ALEX WALKER.

OS: REALLY? FINE BOY, THAT ALEX. KNOWN HIM SINCE HE WAS FIVE OR SIX

YEARS OLD. DO YOU RIDE MUCH, MR. KING?

DK: CALL ME DAKOTA. I TRY TO DO FIFTY MILES A DAY. I'M GETTING IN SHAPE FOR THE ARCADIA NATIONAL.

OS: IS THAT SO? MY SHOP IS SPONSORING ONE OF THE TEAMS. I GUESS THAT MEANS YOU'LL BE RACING AGAINST US.

DK: MR. SHAW, DO YOU KNOW ABOUT ALEX'S NEW BIKE?

OS: KNOW ABOUT IT? HE BOUGHT IT FROM ME.

DK: IT WAS STOLEN NIGHT BEFORE LAST.

OS: STOLEN! THE POOR KID! HE WAITED TWO MONTHS FOR THAT BIKE TO ARRIVE.

DK: WELL, IT'S GONE NOW, AND IT WON'T BE EASY TO FIND. I THOUGHT YOU MIGHT BE ABLE TO HELP.

OS: ME? HOW CAN I HELP?

DK: I WANTED TO ASK YOU SOME QUESTIONS ABOUT YOUR TRIP TO THE AIRPORT THE OTHER DAY WITH ALEX.

OS: MY TRIP TO THE AIRPORT? WHY? WHAT DOES THAT HAVE TO DO WITH ALEX'S BIKE BEING STOLEN?

DK: MAYBE NOTHING. BUT I'D LIKE TO KNOW A FEW THINGS.

OS: ALL RIGHT. LET'S GET IT OVER WITH. I DON'T HAVE MUCH TIME, MR. KING. [ALL OF THE SUDDEN, SHAW WAS NO LONGER THE PLEASANT MAN I HAD BEEN TALKING TO.]

DK: IT'S DAKOTA. ALEX SAID YOU SEEMED VERY NERVOUS ON THE WAY TO THE AIRPORT. AND HE SAID YOU GOT EVEN MORE NERVOUS AT THE CUSTOMS AREA.

OS: NERVOUS? I DON'T KNOW THAT I WAS NERVOUS. I WAS A LITTLE

UNCOMFORTABLE ABOUT HAVING THE BOY ALONG WITH ME.

DK: MAY I ASK WHY?

OS: CUSTOMS AGENTS ARE NOT MY FAVORITE PEOPLE IN THE WORLD, MR. KING. I KNOW THEY'RE ONLY DOING THEIR JOB. BUT THEY CAN MAKE LIKE VERY DIFFICULT FOR SOMEONE WHO DEALS IN IMPORTED GOODS.

DK: DO YOU ALWAYS PICK UP YOUR OWN CARGO AT THE AIRPORT?

OS: NO, MY IMPORTING AGENT USUALLY DELIVERS BIKES TO ME FROM THE AIRPORT. SOMETIMES, WHEN IT'S A SMALL SHIPMENT, I GO MYSELF...UH... TO SAVE THE DELIVERY FEE. [HE SMILED.]

DK: ALEX SAID HE HAD TO WORK HARD TO CONVINCE YOU TO LET HIM COME WITH YOU.

OS: WELL, OF COURSE. I DIDN'T WANT HIM ALONG. I LIKE TO PICK UP MY STUFF AND GET OUT AS SOON AS POSSIBLE. THE LONGER YOU HANG AROUND THERE, THE MORE CHANCE THERE IS THAT YOU'LL GET BOGGED DOWN IN RED TAPE.

DK: AND IS THAT WHY YOU WERE SO FIDGETY IN THE CUSTOMS AREA? WHY YOU WERE LOOKING AROUND, AS THOUGH YOU THOUGHT YOU WERE BEING WATCHED?

OS: LISTEN, KING, ARE YOU INTERROGATING ME, OR WHAT? I THOUGHT YOU WERE HERE FOR A FRIENDLY CONVERSATION. I DON'T HAVE TO ANSWER QUESTIONS LIKE THESE. JUST WHAT ARE YOU GETTING AT, ANYWAY?

DK: I'M NOT GETTING AT ANYTHING, MR. SHAW. I'M JUST TRYING TO FIND OUT WHERE ALEX'S NEW BIKE IS.

OS: WELL, YOU WON'T GET ANY INFORMATION AROUND HERE. I ORDERED THE BIKE FOR HIM IN MAY. HERE'S THE SHIPPING INVOICE TO PROVE IT. I HELPED

HIM ASSEMBLE THE BIKE AT THE AIRPORT. AND I HAVEN'T SEEN IT SINCE.
NOW, IF YOU'LL EXCUSE ME, I HAVE WORK TO DO.

DK: RIGHT. SEE YOU AT THE RACE, MR. SHAW.

END OF TRANSCRIPT

****

CLUE #4

Shaw's Cycle Shop

Date of Order 28 May

Shipped By Europort Ltd.   Date 27 July

Received By O. Shaw

QUANTITY	DESCRIPTION	WEIGHT
3	blue LeMans racing bikes	32 lbs. each
1	red Riviera racing bike	**27 lbs.**
1	red Parisian racing bike	30 lbs.
1	silver Prix racing bike	24 lbs.

* * * *   * *
! ! ! ! ! !

COMPUTER CONVERSATION

- GOOD MORNING, HANDSOME. I SEE YOU GOT MY MESSAGE.

- YES, ZAN. I JUST GOT BACK FROM MY DAILY RIDE. HOW DID YOU MAKE OUT ON THOSE QUESTIONS I ASKED?

- JUST AS I ALWAYS DO: SUCCESSFULLY.

- TELL ME WHAT YOU FOUND.

- THAT 800 NUMBER YOU GAVE ME IS REGISTERED IN THE NAME OF ROEBLING IMPORTS.

- WHAT DO THEY IMPORT?

- ALL KINDS OF THINGS. THEY'RE OWNED BY A LARGER COMPANY CALLED HOLLIS INDUSTRIES.

- WHAT DOES HOLLIS DO?

- AS FAR AS I COULD FIND OUT, THEY JUST OWN OTHER COMPANIES. HOLLIS ALSO OWNS EUROPORT, LTD., **AN EXPORTING COMPANY THAT OPERATES IN HOLLAND AND FRANCE.** THE FRENCH COMPANY RECENTLY SENT SEVERAL SHIP-MENTS OF BIKES TO THE U.S. THEY ARRIVED HERE ON JULY 26, 27, AND 28.

- HOW WERE THESE BIKES SHIPPED, ZAN?
- BY AIR. NOW FOR CADENCE PROPERTIES. THEY ALSO SEEM TO BE A COMPANY THAT OWNS COMPANIES THAT OWN OTHER COMPANIES. A CONGLOMERATE THAT'S IN THE BUSINESS OF BEING IN BUSINESS. THEY DON'T MAKE ANYTHING OR PERFORM ANY SERVICE. THEY JUST BUY AND SELL COMPANIES. AND TALK ABOUT <u>SECRET</u>. I HAVEN'T BEEN ABLE TO FIND A SINGLE THING ABOUT THEIR HOLDINGS. . . .YET.
- KEEP WORKING ON IT, ZAN. YOU'VE DONE GREAT WORK SO FAR. WHAT WOULD I EVER DO WITHOUT YOU?
- I DON'T EVER INTEND TO GIVE YOU A CHANCE TO FIND OUT, LOVE.
- LEAVE AN INVOICE AFTER I SIGN OFF. I'LL TRANSFER THE MONEY TO YOUR CHECKING ACCOUNT LATER TODAY. THANKS, ZAN.
- MY PLEASURE, TARZAN. TALK TO YOU SOON.

END OF COMPUTER CONVERSATION

"I'm outta here, Boss!"

DAKOTA KING
AGENT AT LARGE

MEMORANDUM

TO: Dakota King
FROM: Longh Gonh
CONCERNING: LICENSE PLATE

As I was doing my yoga exercises this morning, I began thinking of our conversation with Alex Walker yesterday. Something that Alex said was dancing around in the back of my mind, but I could not get it to stand still so I could think about it. Then I began running the transcript through my mind. When I reached Alex's statement about the Italian movie star, I had found what I was looking for. Surely there would have been pictures taken of him upon his arrival, and surely pictures record more than what the photographer is actually aiming for.

I went to the library to look at newspapers for July 28, the day after Alex was at the airport. As you know, our library subscribes to several out-of-town newspapers as well as local ones. This wide variety worked very much to my advantage.

I found several articles about the arrival of the Italian movie star Nino Margino and his wife, Anna.

Most of them had pictures. Some of the pictures were taken from the angle I was looking for. One of those pictures showed exactly what I was hoping to find.

Unlike you, of course, I do not travel with a camera in my belt buckle. So I used the library's photocopy machine. For a few extra dimes, I was able to enlarge the picture several times so you could see the background. And then I enlarged again one part of the background, which showed this even more interesting detail.

Study this, Dakota. I will see you this evening. I expect to pursue another lead during the afternoon.

CLUE #5

Dakota King's
Microdiary Entry #6
Re: <u>Two-Wheeled Terror</u>

I hope I never hear anybody in the Z.O.O. crew ask me again why I refuse to work without Longh Gonh. That Italian celebrity fact was in my head as well as his. Obviously great minds think alike. Some great minds just act on things faster than other great minds.

If nothing else, Longh's good work with the newspaper photo proved one thing. Alex certainly wasn't imagining that he had seen the BMW at the airport. And the only solid piece of information we had to work with so far was that the BMW was registered to Cadence Properties. But we still didn't know how Cadence tied into everything else.

It was becoming clear, however, that we were dealing with some sort of international operation. Fact One: Alex's troubles had begun at the customs area of the international section of the airport. Fact Two: Mr. Shaw said that he often went to the airport to pick up his own shipments of bikes. He claimed it was to save the local delivery fee, but his manner raised my doubts. Fact Three: If they weren't just a coincidence, those half-priced imported bikes were another thing that suggested the international scene. None of these were hard facts, of course, but I have learned to regard so-called "coincidence" with some suspicion.

While I was thinking about all this, the front door-bell rang. I flicked on the video camera installed in the wall outside the door. I got a picture of Alex standing outside, waiting for me to answer the door. Then I pressed the ELECTRONIC BUTLER button on my monitor.

I watched the expression on Alex's face as the door swung slowly open. He looked around, trying to find the source of the mechanical voice that said, "Won't you come in, please? Mr. King is waiting in the den for you."

I switched on my own mike. "Relax, Alex," I said. "It's just a little invention I cooked up one rainy day. Come on up. I'm in the room at the top of the stairs."

Alex came up and made himself comfortable on the sofa. "I was just at the cycle shop talking to Mr. Shaw," he said. "He seemed to be mad at me about something."

"I'd stay away from the cycle shop for a while if I were you," I said. "Mr. Shaw got a little steamed at me this morning."

"No kidding? Why?"

"He didn't like the questions I was asking him. In return, I wasn't thrilled with some of his answers."

"I don't get it," Alex said. "Why were you questioning Mr. Shaw? I mean, sure, he seemed a little funny at the airport, but, gosh, I've known him for a long time."

"True," I replied. "And that's exactly why I wanted to talk to him. As Longh would say, 'The end always starts at the beginning,' or something like that. Before your bike was stolen, Mr. Shaw helped you get it."

"But he wouldn't steal—" Alex began.

I interrupted his sentence. "We don't know anything for sure yet, Alex." Then I played the tape of my interview with Orville Shaw and filled Alex in on everything else we'd found out—and hadn't found out—so far.

"Here's an enlarged section from the picture Longh Gonh found in the newspaper," I said, sliding it across the desk.

Alex looked at the photo of the license plate. Then he looked up at me and smiled. "That's the BMW!" he said.

"Right," I answered. "Your suspicions were on target. The car was not only following you around your neighborhood, but as you suspected, it also just happened to be parked outside when you were picking up your bike at the airport."

While I was talking, Alex looked at the original news photo, which Longh had enlarged on the photocopier. He seemed puzzled, did a double-take, then stared at it, wide-eyed. "It can't be!" he said. "That's Mr. Shaw standing by the car. With—with—" he sputtered, pointing at the picture.

"But it is," I said. "I was wondering if you'd notice it. The man you saw standing near the silver car at the shopping center was also at the airport."

"Yeah, yeah!" he answered impatiently. "But, Dakota, that *other* guy—the third one!" He pointed to the man wearing a trench coat and smoking a large pipe. "I just saw that guy outside the bike shop!"

Incredible. Three people in the picture. Mr. Shaw, the BMW driver, and a man I thought was an innocent bystander. Suddenly, the third man turns out to be yet another character we have to identify. One thing I didn't like—the possibility that all three were following Alex. He could be in danger, and I wanted to make sure Longh and I kept him out of it!

"Alex," I said, "From now on I want you to check in with me when you leave your house and when you return to it. I have a simple signaling device I'll give you." I dug around the mess on my desk and came up with the gadget—it looks like an ID bracelet. I snapped it around Alex's wrist.

"What is it? An electronic babysitter?" he asked.

"Not exactly, Alex. It's my Dakota King Tracking Device. It sends a signal to a receiver, telling your geographic location. The receiver gets the signal and charts the location back here at the house, on my computer cartographic screen. If you give the danger signal—three sharp beeps—the computer automatically tracks *my* location and signals me on my tracking receiver." While I was explaining this, I had dug out my half of the hook-up and snapped it on my own wrist.

"Sounds complicated," Alex said.

"But it works, and with all these strange characters showing up where you are a little too often, I'll feel better knowing you've got this," I said. "For a while I just want to know where you are at all times."

Alex smiled. "I like you, too," he laughed. "Now back to the picture. Check out that trench coat."

I looked at the coat on the third man in the photo. He had on one of those trench coats you see in the old movies, the kind with flaps front and back and lapels and a collar wide enough to cover a medium-sized elephant.

"That has to be the guy I just saw at Shaw's. I mean, who else besides Bogart wears a coat like that?"

"How long ago were you at the shop?" I asked.

"Ten minutes," he said. "Maybe fifteen."

"How did you get here?"

"Bike. I'm using my old one."

"It's a slim chance," I said, "but maybe he's still around. If he is, I certainly want to talk to him."

We were both on our way out the door.

"Come on," Alex called over his shoulder. "Race you to Shaw's."

On the way out the door, I grabbed the mini-microcomputer I had just finished wiring the night before. I'd fixed up two of them—one for Longh—so that he and I could keep in constant communication. I slipped it into my shirt pocket, and Alex and I left.

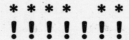

COMPUTER CONVERSATION

● I RECOGNIZE THE FLOWERS, DAKOTA. BUT I THINK THEY'RE MORE APPROPRIATE FOR ZAN THAN FOR YOUR PARTNER.

● SORRY, LONGH. I THOUGHT I'D TRY OUT MY NEW MINI-MICROCOMPUTER. WE'LL HAVE TO WORK OUT OUR OWN SIGN-ON CODE NOW THAT WE HAVE THIS NIFTY LITTLE MACHINE TO CARRY AROUND WITH US. REMEMBER TO ALLOW SOME TIME BETWEEN MESSAGES. THIS SCREEN IS SO SMALL IT CAN ONLY DISPLAY SEVEN LETTERS AT A TIME—IT TAKES A

WHILE TO COMPLETE EACH MESSAGE.

● THAT WILL MAKE YOU CONCENTRATE MORE. WHERE ARE YOU CALLING?

● SHAW'S CYCLE SHOP. ALEX AND I CAME RACING DOWN HERE AFTER HE DISCOVERED YET ANOTHER FASCINATING TWIST TO THIS BICYCLE CASE. THAT PHOTO YOU COPIED FROM THE NEWSPAPER INCLUDES A BONUS. THERE'S A THIRD MAN, STANDING NEXT TO OUR FRIENDLY BMW DRIVER. ALEX SAW THIS GUY OUTSIDE SHAW'S A FEW MINUTES BEFORE HE CAME TO SEE ME.

● VERY PUZZLING. IS HE STILL THERE?

● NO. WE'LL HAVE TO WAIT UNTIL TOMOR-ROW TO SEE IF SHAW CAN TELL US ANYTHING ABOUT HIM. HOW ABOUT YOU, LONGH? WHAT HAVE YOU BEEN UP TO?

● THE 22ND FLOOR OF THE WATSON BUILDING.

● WHAT??

● I SPENT THE AFTERNOON WASHING WIN-DOWS AT THE WATSON BUILDING, WHERE CADENCE PROPERTIES HAS ITS HEAD-QUARTERS. I BORROWED YOUR ZOOM-LENS EYEGLASSES FOR THE OCCASION. FROM MY

SCAFFOLD, I WAS ABLE TO READ SEVERAL MEMOS AND PIECES OF MAIL. WHAT I WANTED WAS TO LEARN WHAT KIND OF BUSINESS CADENCE IS IN.

- WHAT DID YOU FIND OUT?

- NOTHING WE CAN USE. TRANSMITTALS, LETTERS OF CREDIT, STOCK TRANSFERS, AND A MOUNTAIN OF OTHER PAPERWORK. I HAVEN'T A CLUE TO WHAT THEY DO.

- WELL, ZAN IS STILL WORKING ON IT. WE'LL SEE WHAT SHE COMES UP WITH.

- I DID FIND ONE THING THAT SEEMED TO BE IMPORTANT, THOUGH I CAN'T FIGURE OUT WHAT IT MEANS. ON SIX DIFFERENT PIECES OF CORRESPONDENCE, I SAW TWO NUMBERS. EACH TIME, THE NUMBERS WERE PRINTED IN THE CENTER OF THE PAGE, WITH NO OTHER MESSAGE. THE NUMBERS WERE 577704 AND 335.

- OFF THE TOP OF MY HEAD, THEY DON'T MEAN A THING. I'M GOING TO RIDE HOME WITH ALEX NOW. SEE YOU IN ABOUT AN HOUR, LONGH.

END OF COMPUTER CONVERSATION

Dakota King's
Microdiary Entry #7
Re: <u>Two-Wheeled Terror</u>

I told Alex I'd meet him at his house the next morning at seven. We had agreed to pay a visit to Cadence ourselves late in the morning. I figured Alex could accompany me on my daily fifty miles or whatever fraction of it he could sustain. When I stepped out of my house at six-thirty, I realized how eager Alex was to join me. He was sitting next to his bike at the curb, sipping a container of chocolate milk.

"Morning, Dakota," he said brightly. "I woke up early, so I thought I'd come and get you."

"Good," I said. "We can talk business later. When I ride, I like to concentrate on what I'm doing."

"Me, too," Alex said.

"Remember what I told you yesterday," I said. "If you can't keep up, I'll meet you back here at about ten."

"Right," Alex said, and we took off.

I watched Alex's back for the first couple of miles. "He doesn't know much about pacing himself," I thought. "He's going to use up all his energy in the first ten miles."

By the time we had done twenty miles, I had a different idea. Alex was still ahead of me, and he showed no signs of tiring. The kid was in much better shape than I had imagined possible. I began formulating some new plans for next week's bike race. Longh and I had planned on racing as a two-man team. I had just discovered our third rider.

When we hit fifty miles, we eased off and coasted to the downtown business section. After we had cooled down, we locked up the bikes and went into the Watson Building.

We rode up to the 22nd floor, where the elevator doors opened onto an office that took up the whole floor. A receptionist sat at a desk that separated the elevators from the rest of the floor. Alex and I walked up to her, and I went into our prepared script.

"We're looking for Cadence Records," I said.

"This is Cadence Properties," the woman said pleasantly.

"I know," I said. "But I was given this address for Cadence Records."

"It may be one of our companies," she said. "Just a moment, and I'll look it up."

She walked away and disappeared around the corner. As soon as she was gone, Alex and I did the two things we had come up there to do. I slowly scanned the office, trying to memorize every possible detail in case I needed to come back after hours.

Alex bent down and reached into the wastebasket. It was filled with discarded papers, memos, and notes. I was hoping it would include some clue to the kind of business they did in this place.

Alex stuffed most of the paper into his backpack, slid the wastebasket back to where it had been, and slipped the pack onto his back. As he did all this, I saw a man turn a corner and head for the reception area. I could feel the blood drain from my face.

"Alex!" I whispered. "Get out of here!"

"What?" Alex asked, smiling.

"GET OUT!" I whispered louder. I pointed to the door leading to a stairway. "Now! I'll meet you downstairs!"

Alex could see that I wasn't kidding. Within a few seconds, he was out the door and gone. Just as the door closed behind him, the man I had seen came up to the receptionist's desk.

No doubt about it. This was the driver of the silver BMW, possibly the man who had stolen Alex's bike.

"Hello, Mr. Murchison," the receptionist said as she came back to her desk.

"Morning," he said. "Any messages for me?"

She looked through a pile of notes on her desk, pulled one out, and handed it to him. As it passed under my nose, I read the name <u>Leonard Murchison</u>. He took the note without comment and walked away.

"I'm sorry, sir," the woman said, smiling at me. "I've just checked a list of our current holdings, and we don't own any company called Cadence Records."

"How do you like that?" I said, trying to sound disappointed. "I guess someone just gave me the wrong address." We exchanged smiles, and I rang for the elevator.

When I met Alex in the lobby, I told him about the driver of the BMW, Murchison, showing up at Cadence. What a near miss! If he'd seen Alex there the game would have been over for us. Now it was more important than ever to check out the contents of Alex's backpack, which I did when I got back home.

At first glance the wastebasket stuff all looked like what it was—just a bunch of trash. Then as I looked closer certain things stood out and were familiar. There it was again—**Holland.** I'd seen that before, twice in fact: once on the torn label of the tool bag and again on the shipping invoice at Shaw's bike shop. And one more item stood out clearly—**those numbers again—**517704 335—the ones Longh had spotted with the zoom-lens eyeglasses when he was washing windows at Cadence. (I was also glad to see he'd billed them for his window-washing time instead of me!)

All this trash could turn out to be a treasure of clues. I decided my next move would be to visit the bike shop again, to see if these clues would lead me to anything meaningful there.

CLUE #6

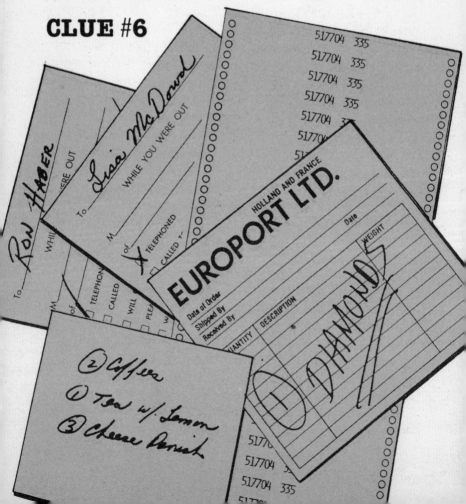

Dakota King's
Microdiary Entry #8
Re: Two-Wheeled Terror

I had a couple reasons now for wanting to talk with Orville Shaw again. The more information we put together, the more suspicious that whole airport scene began to look. More important, I wanted to find out about the guy with the trench coat. He must have had a reason for being both at the airport and the cycle shop. I wasn't about to chalk it up as simple coincidence.

I switched on my microrecorder, opened the door, and walked into the store. Shaw was setting up a display of English racers.

****

TRANSCRIPT

DK: MORNING, MR. SHAW.

OS: OH. MR. KING, ISN'T IT? ALEX'S FRIEND?

DK: DAKOTA, SIR. DAKOTA KING, AS YOU'LL REMEMBER.

OS: I WOULD HAVE THOUGHT YOU'D USED UP ALL YOUR QUESTIONS THE OTHER DAY, MR. KING.

DK: THOSE QUESTIONS, YES. BUT NOW I HAVE A FEW NEW ONES.

OS: Well, what is it this time?

DK: Alex was here to see you last night.

OS: Yes. He left just before I closed up.

DK: And just as someone was coming into the store.

OS: You mean the **Englishman with the pipe?**

DK: Englishman?

OS: Yes, now what did he say his name was? Lew something. Sorelson. That's it, Lew Sorelson.

DK: Lew Sorelson. What was he looking for, Mr. Shaw?

OS: Looking for? A bike, naturally. He looked over our English models. Asked a few questions, then left.

DK: What kind of questions?

OS: Oh, I don't remember, King. He wanted to know if I import any bikes from Japan. How often I get in a new shipment of bikes from Europe. Who my importing agent is. That sort of thing.

DK: I see. By the way, who is your importing agent, Mr. Shaw?

OS: You, too? There seems to be an awful lot of interest in them all of a sudden. I deal with **Roebling Imports.** Been dealing with them for years.

DK: Thanks, Mr. Shaw. See you at the race.

OS: That's what you said last time, Mr. King. Somehow, it seems you never can wait to see me at the race.

DK: Yeah...well.... In closing, let me just say, I'm outta here.

END OF TRANSCRIPT

****

Lew Sorelson. I wanted to do some checking on that guy for sure! The first thing I did when I got home was put a call in to Zan. She was ready for me.

* * * * *   *
! ! ! ! ! !

COMPUTER CONVERSATION

● HELLO, TARZAN. I WAS JUST ABOUT TO CALL YOU. I'VE GOT SOME DATA FOR YOU ON CADENCE PROPERTIES.

● THANKS, ZAN, BUT I PROBABLY WON'T NEED IT. I THINK I KNOW ALL I HAVE TO KNOW ABOUT THEM FOR NOW. HOLD ON TO THAT INFO. I MAY ASK YOU FOR IT LATER.

● IT'S ALREADY STORED IN MY PERMA-NENT TARZAN DATA BANK.

● I NEED SOMETHING ELSE, THOUGH. PLEASE GET ME WHATEVER YOU CAN ON LEONARD MURCHISON, WHO WORKS FOR CADENCE, AND ON AN ENGLISHMAN NAMED LEW SORELSON. HE MIGHT HAVE COME INTO THE COUNTRY ON JULY 27.

● I'VE ALREADY ENTERED THE NAMES ON MY SUBSIDIARY KEYBOARD.

● THANKS, ZAN.

END OF COMPUTER CONVERSATION

Excitement Wheels Into Arcadia

Bike Race Preparations Heat Up

By Alan Loeb/Arcadia Times

Arcadia, August 1—Preparations for the first annual Arcadia National Bike Race were well under way this afternoon, as teams began to arrive from all over the U.S., and even from Canada and Mexico. Orville Shaw, owner of Shaw's Cycle Shop and one of the major local sponsors of the race, watched as his team took a trial run around the oval track.

Arcadia High School has donated the use of its athletic field and grandstands for the race. Local merchants have promised to supply outfits for the riders, standby medical personnel, and transportation for senior citizens who live within a fifty-mile radius of the school.

Neil Chaney, lead rider of the team being fielded by Roebling Imports, told the *Times* of the excitement within his company. "We think we have a pretty good chance to win the race," Mr. Chaney said. "My backup riders, **Murch and Danny,** have both been racing for eight years or more."

Other corporations fielding teams include Cropp's Super-market, Fliegel Brokerage, and Howe Computers. In addition, the race will include several unsponsored teams, whose hopes are just as high as those of the corporate riders.

One of these teams, Team No. 6, includes Alex Walker, who was the *Arcadia Times* Paperboy of the Year two years ago. Alex will be riding with two adults, Dakota King and Longh Gonh. Mr. King told the *Times* he has been practicing for weeks, riding at least fifty miles a day and working to improve his "grasp of the absolutes" of bicycle racing. Mr. Gonh was not available for comment.

Tickets for the race may be purchased at the Town Hall, the post office, and many stores in the downtown shopping mall. The race begins at noon next Saturday.

COMPUTER REPORT #1

- **SUBJECT:** MURCHISON, LEONARD
- **AGE:** 26
- **PRESENT OCCUPATION:** CHAUFFEUR FOR EXECUTIVES OF CADENCE PROPERTIES
- **PREVIOUS OCCUPATIONS:** NONE
- **MILITARY SERVICE:** U.S. MARINE CORPS, SPECIAL SERVICES. MEMBER OF ANTI-TERRORIST ATTACK TEAM, SPECIALIST IN DRIVING VARIOUS TYPES OF VEHICLES, INCLUDING HELICOPTERS. TRAINED IN JUDO, KARATE, AND SEVERAL OTHER MARTIAL ARTS. DISHONORABLE DISCHARGE FOR PHYSICAL ATTACK ON A SUPERIOR OFFICER.
- **ADDITIONAL INFORMATION:** SERVICE RECORD SHOWS OUTSTANDING PERFORMANCE UNTIL A FIGHT IN WHICH MURCHISON SEVERELY BEAT A LIEUTENANT, LEADING TO PRISON AND DISHONORABLE DISCHARGE. HIRED BY CADENCE TWO MONTHS AFTER RELEASE FROM PRISON AS PART OF THE PROGRAM TO HIRE AND TRAIN EX-CONVICTS. DEVOTED TO HIS WORK. OFTEN WORKS 18-HOUR DAY.

COMPUTER REPORT #2

- **SUBJECT:** SORELSON, LEWIS
- **PRESENT OCCUPATION:** MEDICAL SUPPLIES SALESMAN.
- **PREVIOUS OCCUPATIONS:** TYPEWRITER SALESMAN, PERFUME SALESMAN, PERFUME IMPORTER
- **ADDITIONAL INFORMATION:** VISITING U.S. FOR PLEASURE ON TRAVEL VISA, GOOD UNTIL AUGUST 15TH. DOES NO BUSINESS HERE AND HAS NO RELATIVES IN THIS COUNTRY.
- SORRY THIS IS SO BRIEF, HONEY, BUT I KEPT RUNNING INTO DEAD ENDS WITH THIS SORELSON FELLOW. IF I TURN UP ANYTHING MORE SUBSTANTIAL, I'LL GET IT RIGHT TO YOU.

AS FOR THE MURCHISON LAD, HE SOUNDS LIKE TROUBLE TO ME. I HOPE YOU'RE NOT GOING TO GET TOO CLOSE TO HIM. IF YOU DO, PLEASE BE CAREFUL.

LOVE AND XXXXXX'S

ZAN

END OF COMPUTER REPORTS

"I'm outta here, Boss!"

DISAPPEARING INC.

DAKOTA KING
AGENT AT LARGE

MEMORANDUM

TO: Dakota King
FROM: Longh Gonh
CONCERNING: Numbers

There is an ancient Eastern proverb that says: "You cannot contemplate the universe until you fully understand a blade of grass." I remind myself of that proverb whenever I am trying to figure out a problem that seems to have no solution. It sometimes helps to ignore the big picture and to look at the tiniest details.

So it is with the question of the two numbers that have cropped up on various pieces of Cadence paper. I spent hours at the computer trying to find a relationship between the two: 517704 and 335.

I multiplied, divided, added, subtracted, and factored the numbers until I was beginning to get dizzy. No matter what math operation I performed on them, I got results that had no meaning and showed no pattern.

Then, just for a change of pace, I began repeating the same operations on my pocket calculator. Still no progress. But the small screen made me think of the proverb and its advice to concentrate on details, leaving the big picture for another time.

I began to think about the numbers themselves. Never mind the amounts they stood for. Just concentrate on the numbers. I alternated punching in 517704 and 335, staring at the calculator display. As often happens when one concentrates intensely enough, the answer came to me in a flash.

It will come to you, too, Dakota, if you concentrate. Because I am your friend, I will not deprive you of the pleasure of discovery by telling you what the numbers mean. If you **approach the clue from the correct angle,** you will see the hidden meaning of the numbers. Then you will be very pleased with yourself.

The pieces of the puzzle are finally beginning to fit together.

CLUE #7

**Dakota King's
Microdiary Entry #9**
Re: Two-Wheeled Terror

This morning, Alex, Longh Gonh, and I got a taste of what Saturday's race is going to be like. The track was available for test runs today, and at least one representative of each team was there. Each team had twenty minutes to try out the track and get a feel for sprinting, changing riders, and a dozen other things I've been looking forward to for months.

I also wanted to try out some of the techniques Longh had taught me during our training. He had agreed to team up with me for the race only if I mastered the concentration skills he used all the time for endurance tests.

We'd ride out of town on a fifty-mile jaunt, and Longh would chant the phrases he said helped him push his body beyond its limits. I was skeptical at first. But by the third time out, my legs began to feel like pistons, working almost independently of the rest of my body. Once again, Longh had turned out to be right. Now I'd have a chance to try the technique on the race track itself.

Only one rider on the Roebling team showed up, but it wasn't our friend Leonard Murchison. Mr. Shaw stopped by, but he talked only to Alex. He said it was too bad Alex wouldn't be able to race with his new bike. Did he throw a guilty glance in my direction as he said it? I think he did, but I try not to draw conclusions on such flimsy bits of evidence.

When we had finished our twenty-minute run, I was feeling terrific—ready to start the race right then. I hopped off the bike and sat on the ground to tighten one of my shoelaces. Longh was already walking the bike toward the exit gate.

I finished with my laces and looked up into the stands. "It's him!" I said out loud.

"Who?" Alex asked, looking down at me.

I pointed to the stands. "Sorelson!" I said. "And he's on the way out."

I ran and caught up with Longh, grabbed the bike from him, and pedaled to the other side of the field. Sorelson had already left the stands. I pedaled around the stands into the parking lot. Several cars were pulling out, and I didn't see Sorelson anywhere.

Hoping to find him driving one of the moving cars, I raced toward the parking lot exit. But the road outside the school grounds is a limited-access highway with no traffic lights for three miles. The cars were out of sight before I could catch up with the slowest of them.

"Missed him," I said when I got back to Alex and Longh. "What do you suppose he was doing here?"

"I don't know," Alex said. "Who is he, anyway?"

Longh and I looked at each other. Except for the few facts dug up by Zan, all of them useless, we didn't know who he was. The only thing we were now sure of was that it couldn't be mere coincidence that he showed up at the customs office, the cycle shop, and the site of the race.

What was Sorelson looking for? What did he want?

"I'm outta here, Boss!"

DISAPPEARING INC.

DAKOTA KING
AGENT AT LARGE

MEMORANDUM

TO: The Zookeeper
FROM: Longh Gonh
CONCERNING: Unauthorized entry into offices of
Cadence Properties

Although Dakota normally files reports on our
activities, he is putting in some extra time training
for the race and has asked me to report on tonight's
visit to the above-named location. In honor of the
occasion, Dakota had loaded himself down with
gadgets, all inventions of his own, of course. With
such a wealth of communications devices and our
intimate knowledge of the teachings of Ninja
masters, Dakota and I were well prepared for the
task ahead—gaining access to the offices of Cadence
Properties.

Because this investigation still centered on Alex
Walker's missing bicycle, Dakota agreed to let the
boy take part in our plan. Although I disapproved at
first, I was persuaded after Dakota assured me that
Alex would be involved in nothing that was either
dangerous or legally questionable.

Alex, then, would serve as a lookout. He and Dakota wore matching Dakota Two-Way Radio Wristbands, an invention of Dakota's that we have not used for years. If Alex saw anything that looked threatening, he was to notify Dakota immediately. We left him sitting at a bus stop across from the Watson Building.

We entered the building through the locked service entrance. Dakota used his patented Electronic Dakota Decoder to read the security code inside the computerized lock. We punched the code into the number pad, and the door slowly swung open. Before entering we both looked around, then we proceeded.

The service entrance led to the back stairs. We climbed the twenty-two flights to avoid the possibility that a watchman might hear an elevator. Dakota had much less trouble with the stairs than he normally would have. It appears his bicycle training is actually doing him some good. His legs moved swiftly and noiselessly. We reached our destination at the same time with breath to spare.

Another coded lock faced us at the entrance to the Cadence offices. The Dakota Decoder did its job, and we were soon inside. We went straight for the file drawers. Within ten minutes, we had found material that seemed to be relevant to our investigation.

Dakota used his belt-buckle camera to snap pictures of anything we thought would be useful. I regret to say that he was less than precise in lining up some of the papers, so you may have some trouble reading them.

CLUE #8

CADENCE PROPERTIES

OWN 5% OR MORE OF VOTING STOCK:

ABACUS CAMERA
CHILTON RESTAURANTS
DRESS FOR SUCCESS
FLAYVA-GREAT
HOLLIS INDUSTRIES
JCMS, INC.
LOU/LIN BOOKS
'PEN AIR CONCERTS
''SS TOOLS
''RPORATION
''NS

LIN BOOKS
'R CONCERTS
'S TOOLS
'ORPORATION
'DUCTIONS

INC.

We left the offices the same way we had come in and quietly went down the stairs. When we reached the first floor, we heard the watchman making his rounds. He was apparently standing outside the door that stood between us and the service entry driveway. We would have to pass by him without being seen. I opened the door a crack and saw him standing with his back to us.

I whispered the Ninja phrase <u>Heng pu.</u> This phrase denotes a technique for moving behind someone without being seen. It is one of the Secrets of Invisibility all Ninja warriors must master.

"Out of sight, out of mind," Dakota whispered back, using the English translation of the technique we were about to put into effect.

I opened the door wider, and we slipped outside. We stood behind the guard, close enough to touch him. We both concentrated our gaze on the base of his skull, the best way to predict someone's movements. As he moved, so did we, directly behind him. Then, when he turned to go inside, we used the cat-steps of a Ninja warrior and quickly made our way to the street.

When we reached the bus stop, we were astonished to find that Alex was no longer there. We both . . .

(Dakota entered the room at this point and decided to finish this report. What follows is his microdiary report. L.G.)

Dakota King's
Microdiary Entry #10
Re: Two-Wheeled Terror

. . . I'm back from my ride, Boss. I'll take it from here.

When I realized Alex wasn't at the bus stop—wasn't anywhere in the vicinity—I got plenty worried. Here was a kid who trusted me to find his bike, and now *he* was missing!

I shook my wrist hard, hoping Alex would come in on the little wrist radio with a simple explanation of his whereabouts. Nothing but static.

"Why didn't he call me on the radio?" I asked Longh.

"Perhaps he will communicate soon," Longh answered. "We must commence our search immediately and within range of his radio."

At that precise moment, my own radio crackled. When I held it to my ear, I heard two distinctly unfamiliar voices coming out of it.

"Are all these bikes ready for shipment?" one voice asked.

"I don't think so," a deeper voice answered. "They told me to hold up until I get the official word. There's some kind of problem with one or two of them."

The two men kept talking, but Longh and I

couldn't hear what they were saying. Apparently, they were walking away from Alex's wrist radio.

The next thing we heard was my name being whispered over the radio.

"Dakota?"

"Alex?" I whispered to my wrist.

"Shhh!" he hissed. "Listen! I'm in some kind of warehouse or garage. The place is filled with bikes. I followed Murchison here, and he met another guy. Wait, wait! They're coming back!"

Now we heard footsteps. Then one of the voices said, "I'm telling you, I heard somebody talking. There he is!"

Shuffling, some crashing sounds, then the second voice yelled, "Grab that kid before he gets away!"

Then the radio went dead.

Longh pointed to the parking lot next to the building we had just come out of. "This way!" he said.

As we ran, he kept checking the dial on the DK Radio Tracker that he had remembered to bring with him. I invented that one some years back, and it had never come in handier than right now. Longh followed the dial, and I followed him, until we were standing outside a door under a sign that said MAINTENANCE GARAGE.

Now we could hear the crashing noises first-hand as the men threw aside heavy crates and boxes to search for Alex. We had to get in there before they succeeded.

The garage door was held shut by a huge padlock. My Decoder wouldn't help us with that. Longh knelt in front of the door and took the lock in his hands.

I had seen Longh do this before, but it still amazed me each time. First, he cradled the lock in the palm of his left hand. Then he closed his eyes and gently traced the outline of the lock with his fingers. When his fingers stopped to a certain point on the lock, he firmly pressed them into the metal.

Longh smiled, satisfied that he had found what he needed. He removed his hands from the lock and took one step back. Then he reached out and hit it with the side of his hand.

The lock sprung open. At the same instant, an ear-piercing sound filled the air. It was a siren, and it was coming from inside the warehouse.

"Let's get out of here!" one of the voices cried over the sound of the siren. Longh removed the padlock and slid the door open. The place was dark. We took a few cautious steps into the garage. Then the siren stopped.

I held my breath and stepped over some crates that had been spilled onto the floor. Suddenly, a flashlight beamed on us, and we froze. It was impossible to see who was standing behind that light.

"Nifty little invention, Dakota," Alex said. He lowered the light beam to the floor, and we saw him grinning at us. He was holding the Dakota King Pocket Siren I had given him when he came to visit me.

"Are you all right?" I asked, as we ran up to him.

"I am now that you guys are here," he said.

"What are you doing here?" I asked.

"While I was waiting at the bus stop," Alex said, "I saw a man come out of the building. When he turned in my direction, I recognized him. It was the guy in the BMW."

"Leonard Murchison," Longh said.

"So I figured, why not follow him?" Alex said.

"I can think of roughly a hundred and eleven reasons why not," I said. "You had some trouble with the radio?"

"I think I was pressing the wrong button," Alex answered. "I couldn't get through to you."

"But you followed him anyway?" Longh said.

"Well, sure," Alex said. "Who knew what he might lead me to? Anyway, I stayed far enough behind so he didn't know I was there. He unlocked the outside door and came in without closing it. So I slipped in and hid behind one of those big trucks."

"How did you get locked in?" I asked.

"When he went out, he pulled the door shut and locked it from the outside. Later he came back in through a back door, with another guy. They started talking about the bikes—"

"We know the story from there on," I said. "We were listening in. Do you think they know who you are?"

"I doubt it," Alex said. "I don't think either of them saw my face at all."

"Good," I said. "By the way, what bikes were they talking about?"

"Come and take a look," Alex said, leading us farther into the dark garage. When he got to the wall, he reached up and flipped a light switch.

"How about that?" he said, smiling.

This corner of the garage was filled with racing bikes. There must have been fifty of them, all brand-new.

Alex walked over to them and edged his way up to the red bike. He grabbed the handlebars and wheeled it out to an open space on the floor.

"This," he said happily, "is my bike. And I have the bill of sale to prove it!"

Dakota King's
Microdiary Entry #11
Re: Two-Wheeled Terror

So Alex had his bike back. Now the question was, why was it stolen? I still couldn't believe that a guy like Murchison—let alone a big company like Cadence—would be involved in a ring that did nothing but steal bicycles. What was this really all about?

At this point, all fingers pointed at Murchison. But the next morning, some of those fingers backed off, because of what Longh brought home from the police station. If I ask questions his answers are usually mind exercises meant to make me sharpen my skills in logic. The physical exercise of preparing for the bike race was all I could handle at this point. All that mattered to me was that an important piece of information had just been handed over to me and I was plenty grateful.

I have no idea how he got his hands on the police report. I never ask him about things like that. I just accept these things as gifts.

Look the report over, and you'll see why the Murchison solution was just too simple.

I checked with Alex, and the bike described in the report is his—he was visiting a friend of his on Massey Street.

CLUE #9

ARCADIA POLICE DEPARTMENT
INVESTIGATION REPORT

DATE 4 August

REASON FOR INVESTIGATION Phone call from George Kelp, 184 Massey Street. Informant reported a suspicious-looking person examining a bicycle that was chained to a telephone pole across the street from his home.

RESULT OF INVESTIGATION Officer Abramowitz and I responded to the call within five minutes. We found a red racing bike, bearing the brand name "Riviera," chained to said telephone pole. No one was in the vicinity. Spoke to Mr. Kelp, who had called from his home. Kelp described the man as tall, about 40, wearing trench coat and smoking a pipe. He said the man showed a great deal of interest in the bike, examining it close up from various angles. After a few minutes, the man walked down the street, turned the corner, and did not return. No further investigation seemed to be called for.

OFFICERS FILING THIS REPORT

Patrol Officer Naomi Heaney   Patrol Officer Michael Abramowitz

Dakota King's
Microdiary Entry #12
Re: <u>Two-Wheeled Terror</u>

In some of my toughest cases, the biggest problem is coming up with a likely suspect. Not this one. This time, I felt as though I were surrounded by people who had an abnormal interest in that red racing bike.

Leonard Murchison seemed to be the best bet, but that might have been because I had the most data about him. He had a prison record, and that would have made it hard for him to find a legitimate job. But Cadence Properties hired him. Remember, we had just learned that Cadence owned Hollis Industries. And we already knew that Hollis owned Europort and Roebling, exporters and importers of bikes. We saw Murchison with the bikes in the Cadence garage—well Boss, it's a vague connection, maybe, but that's not to say there's *no* connection. And Murchison liked bikes enough to be involved in the same race we were training for.

Orville Shaw's name was still high up there on my list of suspects. I wasn't ready to buy the explanation he gave me for his nervousness at the airport. I think he was worried about something going wrong. And that picture at the airport that caught the BMW and those three guys—did Shaw just happen to be close by when it was snapped? No, I think all of this has <u>some-</u>

thing to do with the theft of Alex's bike.

And now there was Lew Sorelson, the mystery figure in the trench coat. First he's at the airport. Then he turns up at the cycle shop. Next, he's at the track on a full practice day. To top it all, he's spotted suspiciously eyeing Alex's bike in the street. The man has given us reason to want to get our hands on him and ask him a few pertinent questions.

All of the above, Boss, only left me with more unanswered questions to deal with. What were all those bikes doing in the garage of the Watson Building? What was Murchison doing with them? I couldn't believe he was a simple bike thief. There isn't enough money in that kind of crime.

If Murchison was involved, what did it have to do with Cadence Properties? They certainly weren't stealing bikes for profit. What was their interest in all this?

How did those half-price bikes offered by Roebling tie in with anything? Did Orville Shaw have anything to do with them? Why would he be picking up a shipment of bikes at the airport if he did business with Roebling Imports?

How about that tool bag from Holland?

And just who was Lew Sorelson?

As if I didn't have plenty to think about already, there was a new wrinkle in the deal—a small item in the sports section of the local paper. I like excitement as much as the next guy does, but the article gave me a little more excitement to think about than I really wanted. It sure would be nice to have a little time off from this stuff until after the race, but according to the newspaper that just wasn't going to happen.

Anonymous Caller Hints at Foul Play During Arcadia National

By John Paul Bart/Arcadia Times

Arcadia, August 6—A spokesperson for the Arcadia Police Department said yesterday that security at the Arcadia National Bike Race will be heavier than expected tomorrow. An anonymous phone call was given as the reason for the increased police protection.

"An unidentified male phoned the department last night," the spokesperson said. "He said there was likely to be violence at the athletic field during or after the race. We are not taking any chances."

The mayor announced today that every measure was being taken to assure the safety of everyone at the race, participants and spectators alike. The race will begin at noon tomorrow.

* * * * *   *

! ! ! ! ! ! !

COMPUTER CONVERSATION

- HELLO, GORGEOUS. DID YOU READ THE TWO PROFILES I LEFT FOR YOU?

- SURE DID, ZAN, THANKS.

- I HOPE YOU TOOK MY WARNING SERIOUSLY AND STAYED AWAY FROM THAT MURCHISON GUY.

- BELIEVE ME, I HAVEN'T BEEN NEAR HIM.

- DO YOU WANT ME TO CONTINUE INVESTIGATING CADENCE PROPERTIES?

- AS A MATTER OF FACT, I'M CALLING TO TELL YOU TO DROP THAT ONE. I'VE ALREADY FOUND OUT ALL I NEED TO KNOW ABOUT CADENCE. I'M BEGINNING TO THINK I ALREADY KNOW EVERYTHING I NEED ABOUT THIS WHOLE CASE. BUT I STILL CAN'T GET EVERYTHING TO FIT TOGETHER.

- YOU WILL, SWEET. YOU ALWAYS DO. JUST USE YOUR BRAIN, AS YOU ALWAYS DO. AND BE VERY CAREFUL, AS YOU NEVER ARE.

- WHERE DO I GET THIS REPUTATION FOR RECKLESS DARING? I NEVER DO ANYTHING THAT'S THE SLIGHTEST BIT RISKY. WELL, HARDLY EVER.

- DOES THIS MEAN I'M GOING TO LOSE CONTACT WITH YOU FOR ANOTHER COUPLE OF MONTHS?

- DON'T BE SO PESSIMISTIC. WHO KNOWS WHAT I MIGHT NEED YOU FOR NEXT WEEK?

- I KEEP HOPING YOU'LL NEED ME FOR MORE THAN JUST MODEM MESSAGES. WHEN ARE WE GOING TO GET TOGETHER WITHOUT ALL THIS HARDWARE?

- SOON, ZAN. THANKS FOR YOUR HELP. LEAVE YOUR INVOICE ON MY COMPUTER. I'LL TALK TO YOU SOON.

- YOU KNOW MY CODE. GOOD LUCK IN THE BIKE RACE.

END OF COMPUTER CONVERSATION

Dakota King's
Microdiary Entry #13
Re: <u>Two-Wheeled Terror</u>

We arrived at the track with two hours to spare.
Longh had left his bike at the track the night before.
He jogged there in the morning, just to remind us that
his body is capable of doing things the rest of us think
are impossible. (That wasn't his intention, I know. But
he does have a way of making hard work seem like a
walk to the bus station. And he *did* get to the track
before we did on our bikes.)

The three of us had spent hours the night before
debating who would ride the opening lap. My bike was
unquestionably the easiest to ride, with the new fluid
I'd invented to replace my ball bearings.

On the other hand, Longh's bike was without
doubt the fastest—maybe the fastest bike I've ever
seen, if it has the right rider. Longh claims that it's
merely a matter of keeping a bike well-oiled, clean,
and free from rust. I suspect he has subjected it to
some mystical Oriental rite that he won't tell me about.

Alex's new bike was the only one we weren't sure
about, because we had so little experience with it. At
the race weigh-in station, it came in at **26 pounds.** It
was the heaviest of our three bikes. But we weren't
about to replace it. It was our bait for smoking out the
thief. I was sure two of our three suspects would be at

the race. And I was willing to bet my jet-powered shoes that all three of them would be there. That bike had some powerful attraction for someone, and I was determined to find out what it was.

I didn't have to wait long. About an hour before the race, I was running a last-minute check on my wheels, and Longh was just coming out of a yoga trance he uses to psych himself up before any competition. Alex was behind me, doing some stretching exercises. Suddenly, I heard a familiar voice talking to him.

"Hi. Len Murchison. I've been admiring your bike."

I was dumbfounded. So was Alex, but only for a few seconds. "Thanks," he said, looking Murchison straight in the eye. "It's new. We're just going to break it in today."

"Oh? I thought I saw you riding it a couple of weeks ago," Murchison said casually, one bike rider to another. "I know I've seen it somewhere."

"Uh—it might have been me," Alex said. "Where was it?"

"I really don't remember," Murchison said. "I do a lot of riding around. Well, I have to get back to my team. Good luck."

"Thanks," Alex said. "Same to you." Then he added, under his breath, "I think."

"What do you make of that?" I said to Longh, who had come completely back to the conscious world. "Can you believe the guy could have so much nerve!"

"Careful, Dakota," Longh said patiently. "Remember a prime rule of investigative work—"

"I know, I know," I said. "Never let your preconceptions hinder your search for the facts. But what has that got to do with what just happened?"

"Why are you shocked that Murchison came over to admire Alex's bike?" Longh asked.

"Because he stole it!" Alex blurted out.

"Nope," I said. "Longh is right. That's a preconception, not a fact."

"You mean he didn't steal my bike? But he drives that BMW, and he was at the garage," Alex said.

"I mean," I said, "that we don't know yet who stole your bike. Suppose it wasn't Murchison. Then there wouldn't be anything strange about his coming over to talk to you."

"On the other hand, suppose he is the thief?" Longh asked. "Then our task is to determine what his false show of friendship could mean."

Longh was right, of course. But the whole matter would have to be put off for a while. Preparations for the race were beginning. We had no time for anything now except doing all we could to win.

As we walked our bikes to the starting position, we passed Mr. Shaw and the team he was sponsoring. He looked at Alex's bike, and his eyes widened.

"I see you got it back, Alex," he called. "Did the police find the thief?"

"Not yet," Alex called back.

I leaned closer to him and whispered, "Don't say anything more." Alex smiled and waved to Shaw, and we kept moving.

"There is our third acquaintance," Longh said from behind me. "Look slowly to your right, and you will see Sorelson."

I looked out to my left for a few seconds, then casually turned my head to the right. There he was, trench coat, pipe, and sour look—the same as always.

"Hail, hail," I said, "the gang's all here."

"And one of them would seem to want that bike

back," Longh said.

"Just let them try getting my bike again," Alex said defiantly. "Just let them try."

It occurred to me that Alex might like a permanent souvenir of our race. So I turned on the stopwatch recorder I was wearing around my neck and picked up the announcer.

****

TRANSCRIPT

LADIES AND GENTLEMEN, THE TEAMS ARE IN PLACE, THE FIRST-LAP RIDERS ARE AT THE STARTING LINE, AND THE FIRST ANNUAL ARCADIA NATIONAL BIKE RACE IS ABOUT TO BEGIN. THE RACE WILL CONSIST OF FIFTY COMPLETE LAPS OF THE TRACK, FOR A TOTAL DISTANCE OF SEVENTY-FIVE MILES. EACH RIDER WILL BE REPLACED BY A TEAM MEMBER AT THE END OF EACH LAP.

RIDERS, MOUNT YOUR BIKES. YOU MAY BEGIN AT THE SOUND OF THE STARTING GUN.

THEY ARE OFF, LADIES AND GENTLEMEN! AND AS THEY ROUND THE FIRST TURN, FLIEGEL BROKERAGE, IN A BLUE SHIRT, TAKES AN EARLY LEAD. THAT'S ROEBLING IMPORTS IN BLACK BEHIND HIM, FOLLOWED BY CROPP'S IN RED, INDEPENDENT RIDER FROM TEAM NO. 6 IN WHITE, AND FASTBACK PRESS IN PURPLE.

NOW ROEBLING MOVES AHEAD, AS THE LEAD RIDERS NEAR THE COMPLETION OF THE FIRST LAP. AND HERE COME THE SECOND TIER, TO REPLACE THOSE RIDERS, WHO HAVE JUST DONE A MILE-AND-A-HALF SPRINT IN UNDER TWO MINUTES.

On this second lap, Team No. 6 is moving up fast, and I mean fast. Let's see, my list tells me that first-tier rider Alex Walker has just been relieved by Dakota King. Look at that bike move! Team 6 is now second, right behind Roebling...

****

As the lead riders complete Lap 25, Longh Gonh has opened the lead for Team 6. Roebling is nearly a full lap behind, and the rest of the track is trailing.

Alex Walker is now up for Team 6, and he seems to be maintaining the sizable lead built up by his teammate Longh Gonh. Now Roebling has closed the lead a bit, but Team 6 still has a comfortable lead...

****

Ladies and gentlemen, we have just completed Lap 47, and this exciting race is nearing its climax. Gonh rides up to his teammate Walker, and...what's this? Something seems to be wrong with Team 6. Walker is standing in position, but he is without a bike! Gonh stops and hops off his bike, Walker hops on and pedals away.

Team 6 has now lost a good bit of ground. We have no information about what happened to the red bike Walker was riding. But I don't see how they can maintain their lead this way. If they have to stop to change riders, they'll lose precious seconds on each lap.

Now Team 6 is completing Lap 48, with Roebling hot on their tail. King relieves Walker for Lap 49. Roebling is edging up behind Team 6, which is still riding under the handicap of only

TWO BIKES.

AND NOW WE'RE INTO THE COMPLETION OF THE NEXT-TO-LAST LAP. THAT'S
WALKER WAITING TO RELIEVE KING, EVEN THOUGH THIS LAP BELONGS TO
GONH. WE CAN'T SEE GONH ANYWHERE, NOR DO WE SEE WALKER'S RED
BIKE.

BUT KING RIDES BY WALKER—HE'S GOING TO TAKE THE LAST LAP HIMSELF!
ROEBLING IS RIGHT BEHIND HIM, AND IT'S GOING TO BE A FIGHT TO THE FINISH
BETWEEN TEAM 6 AND ROEBLING IMPORTS!

AS THEY ROUND THE FAR TURN, ROEBLING INCHES UP ON KING, WHO HAS
TO BE EXHAUSTED, RIDING TWO CONSECUTIVE LAPS WITHOUT A BREATHER.
NOW ROEBLING HAS THE LEAD! BUT KING NOSES AHEAD OF HIM AGAIN!

THEY'RE INTO THE FINAL STRETCH, AND IT'S IMPOSSIBLE TO BE SURE WHO'S
AHEAD. THEY'RE RIDING NECK AND NECK. KING NOW HAS A SLIGHT LEAD. NO,
NOT ANYMORE. NOW ROEBLING INCHES AHEAD. NOW IT'S KING. NOW
ROEBLING AGAIN.

AND AS THEY CROSS THE FINISH LINE, DAKOTA KING HAS IT BY LESS THAN
A FOOT! LADIES AND GENTLEMEN, INDEPENDENT TEAM 6 HAS WON THE
FIRST ANNUAL ARCADIA NATIONAL BIKE RACE! AND WHAT A FINISH! WHAT
A SHOW OF STAMINA AND STRENGTH BY DAKOTA KING! ON A TEAM MISSING
ONE RIDER AND ONE BIKE, HE TOOK IT UPON HIMSELF TO FINISH THE RACE.
WHAT A RACE!

DON'T GO AWAY, FOLKS. WE'LL HAVE THE PRESENTATION OF THE TROPHIES
IN JUST A FEW MINUTES.

END OF TRANSCRIPT

****

Dakota King's
Microdiary Entry #14
Re: Two-Wheeled Terror

Well, that tells you how the race went, Boss. Some people might think the announcer overdid it a bit at the end there, but riding those last two laps without relief is every bit as astounding as he made it out to be.

What the announcer and the spectators didn't know is that there was a whole other drama going on under the stands. The police, acting on that anonymous phone call (even I didn't know till now that it had come from Longh), were there in force. But they didn't known what to look for.

Lew Sorelson, on the other hand, did know. He flashed a badge, the police went into action, and Alex's bike was taken into custody right then and there. They weren't taking any chances of the bike being stolen by someone else again.

So now you have everything you need. I went to the trouble of putting this file together for you so you could take action once you figure out just what action needs to be taken, that is. Of course, I wasn't going to deprive you and your agents of the fun of figuring things out—just as Longh and I did.

You guys will be able to put it all together, I'm sure. Then you can put a stop to what we discovered. I'm taking off for a ski trip. On the chance that you may have some trouble, I'll mail you the solution to this mystery from out West. In the meantime, **I'm outta here, Boss!**

FROM:
DAKOTA KING
DEATH VALLEY, CA.

TO:
ZONE OPERATIONS ORGANIZATION
9909 INCOGNITO DRIVE
ARLINGTON, VIRGINIA 90909

I'm outta here, Boss!

D K

And The Villain Is . . .

I would have bet my own racing bike that Leonard Murchison was the man we were after. But the owner of the cycle shop was responsible for the theft—and for a lot more.

Murchison's friendly conversation with Alex before the race turned out to be genuine interest in Alex's bike. He really was just admiring it as an efficient and good-looking machine. He later admitted that he had seen Alex riding the bike the day it arrived and, in fact, had slowed down to get a better look at it. But he had never even seen Alex's face, not even that night in the garage. So it wasn't until they met at the track that Murchison realized that it might have been the same bike.

The incident in the garage turned out to be misleading. Murchison was there with another Cadence employee to check on a shipment of bicycles. All he knew was that Roebling had imported them and would be shipping them out soon. When they spotted Alex, they thought he was a thief, and they went after him. When Alex used his pocket siren, Murchison and friend went for the police. Then Longh and I arrived, but by the time Murchison got back, we had already left the garage.

When I found out that Cadence owned Hollis Industries, which owns Europort and Roebling, I realized that Cadence was connected with those super-discount imported bikes. And somebody at Cadence was obsessed with getting in touch with Hollis. That's what those calculator digits were about. Read upside down on a calculator 335 looks like SEE, and 517704 looks like HOLLIS.

Another thing that aroused my curiosity was one of the scraps Alex dug out of the wastebasket in the Cadence offices. One of their companies—Europort—is in the business of exporting diamonds, along with bicycles, chocolates, and tulip bulbs. And they have another company—Roebling—that imports the same stuff. One of those bicycles appears to have been much more valuable than its purchase price—at least, someone badly wanted to get his hands on it!

So I reasoned that the thief didn't want the bike itself—he wanted something inside it. Why would anyone put something inside a bike? To slip it past customs, of course.

What would be small enough to hide inside a bike, but valuable enough to risk violating the customs law? Chocolates? Tulip bulbs? Try diamonds. And where's the international center for diamond exporting? Try Amsterdam, Holland, where Shaw got his tool bag.

Shaw was involved in smuggling diamonds past customs so they could be disposed of in this country without being traced. Someone over there at Europort would insert the diamonds into the hollow tubes that make up the body of the bike. Then someone here at Roebling would remove the diamonds before the bike was delivered.

So Shaw had good reason for being nervous as this

bike shipment went through customs. He had agreed to let Alex go with him because Alex's bike wasn't supposed to be carrying diamonds. Also, that way he could be sure that Alex's bike was safely out of the way. It wasn't until the next day that Shaw discovered a mistake had been made in Europe.

That made it necessary for him to steal the bike to remove the diamonds. Alex's bike was carrying one pound of the smuggled goods. I knew that because the bike weighed twenty-six pounds at the race, one pound less than the weight given on the shipping invoice. Shaw hid the bike in the Cadence garage at the Watson Building with the rest of the shipment. The diamonds were removed there, and then the bikes were held until Roebling picked them up for delivery.

So every one of those bikes in the garage had been used as a secret transporter of smuggled diamonds, but Alex's was the only one that had already been sold. Since the police were looking for it, my guess is that after the diamonds were removed, Shaw was planning to return the bike to Alex the same way he'd taken it—in the dead of night.

Although Murchison, as a Cadence employee, had nothing to do with all this, Cadence itself is certainly involved. That much is clear from the fact that the Cadence garage is the place where the diamonds are removed. You knew there was some Cadence connection, Boss, when you put me onto the case. I know you people at the Z.O.O. aren't allowed to investigate strictly local matters. That would bring a Congressional committee down on your heads. So I did what you needed me to do. I established that Cadence was involved in something wider than a simple bike theft.

Well, I've done the job for you. Now it's up to you guys to break open the smuggling ring that Shaw—

along with Roebling, Europort, and Cadence—has been operating for some time now.

And Sorelson? You've probably figured out by now that he's with British customs. He never sold a typewriter or a bottle of perfume in his life. That was all a front. Maybe this means the smuggling ring operated in Britain, too, but Zan couldn't get any information on this or on him because the British secret service doesn't want anyone to know anything about him.

I know all of you in the Z.O.O. will do a bang-up job of wrapping it all up. As for your secret, Boss, it's safe with me. Although Alex and I have promised to keep in touch, he will never know his Uncle Ulysses does anything more exciting than selling burglar alarms.

Dakota King

"I'm outta here, Boss!"

Congratulations!

You've solved the case of Two-Wheeled Terror! But you're not finished with your investigating work yet. There are plenty of other files in the exciting Secret Files of Dakota King series.

Now that you've proven yourself to be a case-cracker of the highest quality, you're ready to dig into the other Secret Files of Dakota King. You are requested to join the secret agents at Zone Operations Organization (also known as the Z.O.O.), and help them solve the unsolved cases left behind by that always-on-the-go, agent-at-large, Dakota King. King and Longh Gonh, his partner at Disappearing Inc., are off on yet another exciting adventure. The results of their travels are always the same—files full of clues, transcripts, maps, scraps of paper, sketches, photographs, and who knows what else. Are you ready to face the next case?

Get some rest and plenty of it (you deserve it after Two-Wheeled Terror!) Then get set to tackle more Secret Files of Dakota King. Dakota, Longh, the Zookeeper . . . they're all counting on YOU!

THE SECRET FILES OF
DAKOTA KING

#1 Operation Black Fang

Jake MacKenzie

A secret formula turns out to be a formula for DANGER!

A mysterious plane crash with no survivors and no bodies is just the beginning of this unsolved mystery. Clues in the plane lead Dakota King and his partner Longh Gonh to a closetful of poisonous snakes and a top-secret government laboratory full of suspicious characters.

There's a load of poisonous material missing. Who would steal it? Why would anyone take such desperate risks to get it? Dakota and Longh Gonh are out to find some answers. Using their Ninja skills, Dakota's incredible inventions, and all their finely-tuned investigative skills the two agents-at-large have filled a file full of clues, maps, photographs, and tape recorded conversations for the Zookeeper and YOU to use to solve the mystery.

What is this poison? What's being done with it? Will Dakota get out of this fang-tastic mess alive? All the clues are here in Operation: Black Fang!, file #1 of The Secret Files of Dakota King.

THE SECRET FILES OF
DAKOTA KING

#2 The Haunted City of Gold

Jake MacKenzie

There's a treasure missing and everybody's after it!

Poisoned darts, flying double-edged daggers, haunted statues, and deadly tarantulas make just another day in the jungle just another brush with death for Dakota King and his partner Longh Gonh.

Somewhere deep in the jungles of Paramar, a treasure lost for centuries lies undiscovered. But where? It's King's job to find it, and as his search begins, he quickly discovers that he's not the only one on this treasure hunt! Whoever it is that's on the jungle trail to the treasure wants to make sure that Dakota King never makes it out of this jungle alive.

What is the treasure? Where is it hidden? Who else is after it? And most important of all, will Dakota King get out of this mess in one piece? All the answers are here in The Haunted City of Gold, file #2 of The Secret Files of Dakota King.

THE SECRET FILES OF
DAKOTA KING

#3 Two-Wheeled Terror

Jake MacKenzie

A boy, a bicycle, and somebody's following them both!

Alex Walker's slick, new, foreign racing bike arrives on time, and with it comes big trouble! Strangers start following Alex, his bike is stolen, and he's caught in the middle of a mysterious mess only Dakota King can untangle.

Why would anyone want to steal his bike? Who are the unknown drivers of the fancy BMW car that shows up wherever Alex is? Who is that interesting pipe-smoking man with the English accent? Why is the bike shop owner suddenly so nervous?

Dakota King and Longh Gonh allow Alex to work with them to find clues for this file as all three train for an important bike race. On the track of clues and on the race track, they're a team determined to discover who's responsible for the Two-Wheeled Terror, file #3 of The Secret Files of Dakota King.